This book belongs to:

....

The **RED RECTANGLES**.

No, the **GREEN LIZARDS**.

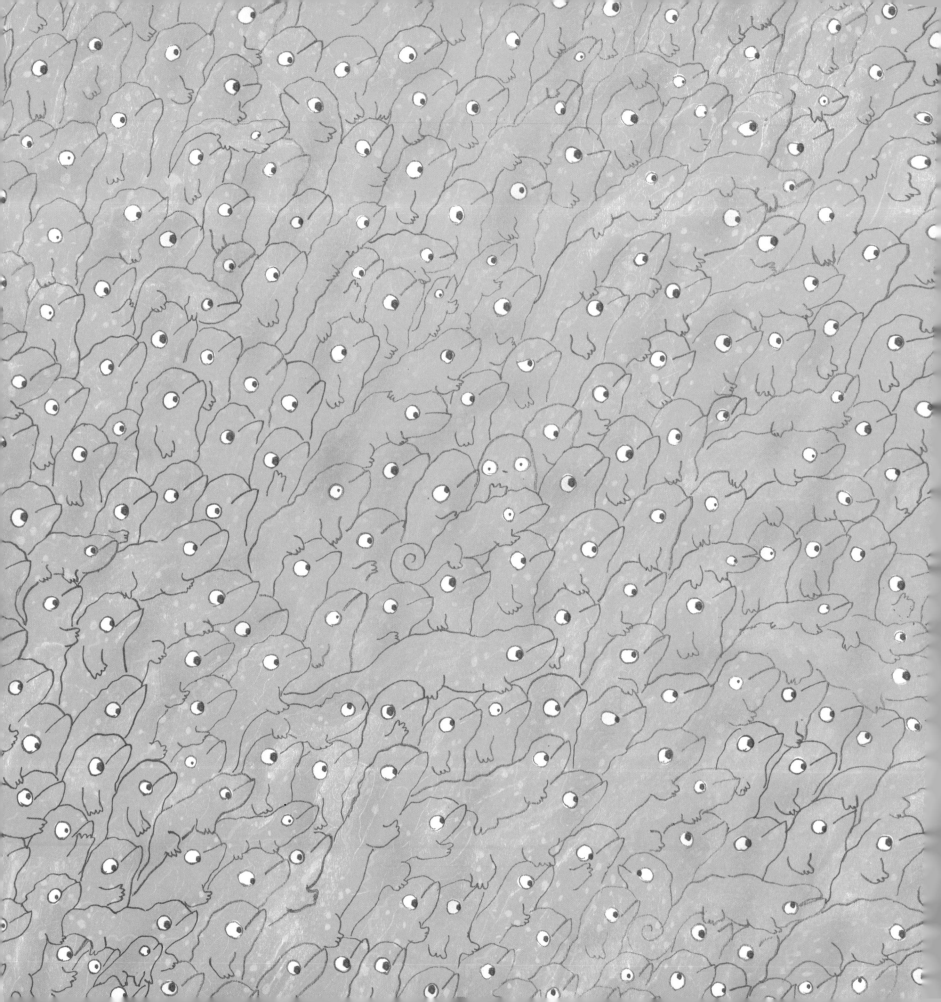

More fantastic books by Steve Antony:

Please Mr Panda
Steve Antony

I'll Wait, Mr Panda
Steve Antony

'This picture book is hard to beat.' *The Times*

THE QUEEN'S HAT
Steve Antony

'This picture book is hard to beat.' *The Times on The Queen's Hat*

THE QUEEN'S HANDBAG
Steve Antony

THE QUEEN'S PRESENT
Steve Antony

For fun activities, further information and to order, visit www.hodderchildrens.co.uk

To my brothers, Kev, Rich and Andy

HODDER CHILDREN'S BOOKS
First published in Great Britain in 2015 by Hodder and Stoughton
This edition published in 2016

A CIP catalogue record for this book is available from the British Library.

ISBN: 978 1 444 92011 6

10 9 8 7 6 5 4 3 2 1

Printed and bound in China

Hodder Children's Books
An imprint of Hachette Children's Group
Part of Hodder and Stoughton
Carmelite House
50 Victoria Embankment
London EC4Y 0DZ

An Hachette UK Company
www.hachette.co.uk
www.hachettechildrens.co.uk

GREEN LIZARDS
VS
RED RECTANGLES

Steve Antony

Hodder Children's Books

The **GREEN LIZARDS** and the **RED RECTANGLES** were at war.

The **GREEN LIZARDS** tried their best to defeat the **RED RECTANGLES,**

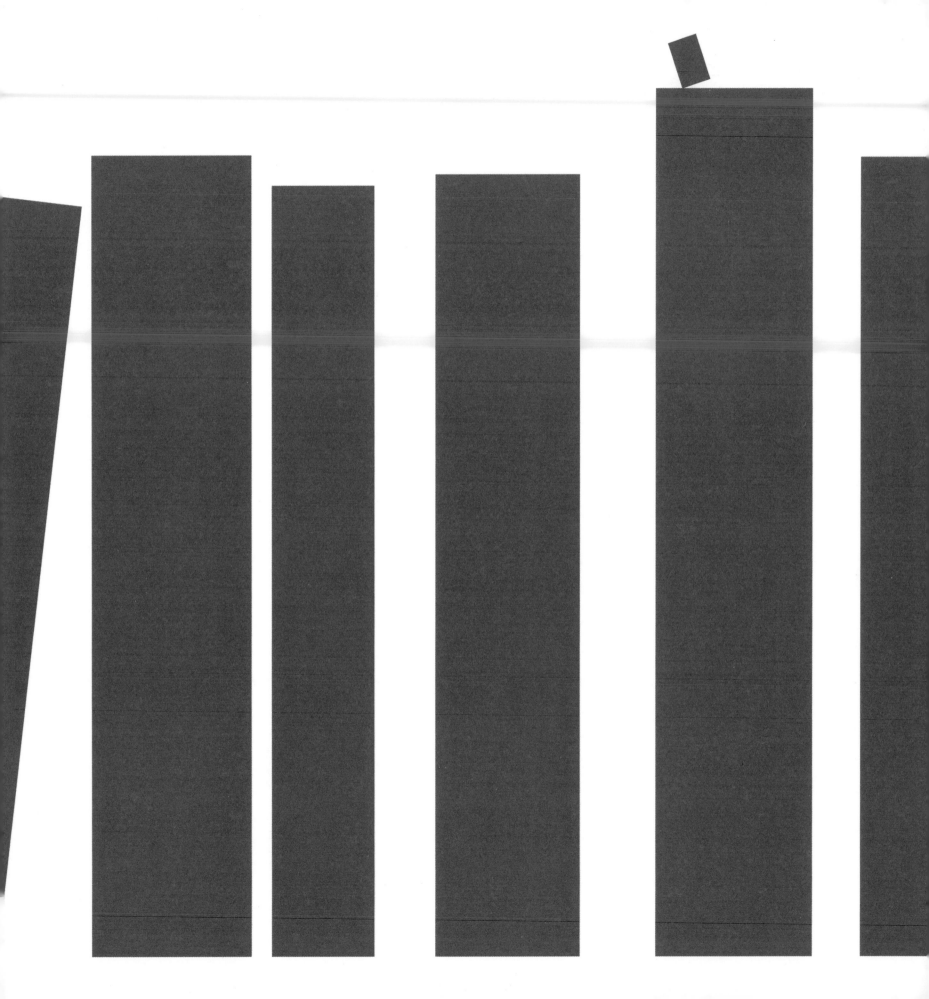

but the **RED RECTANGLES** were smart.

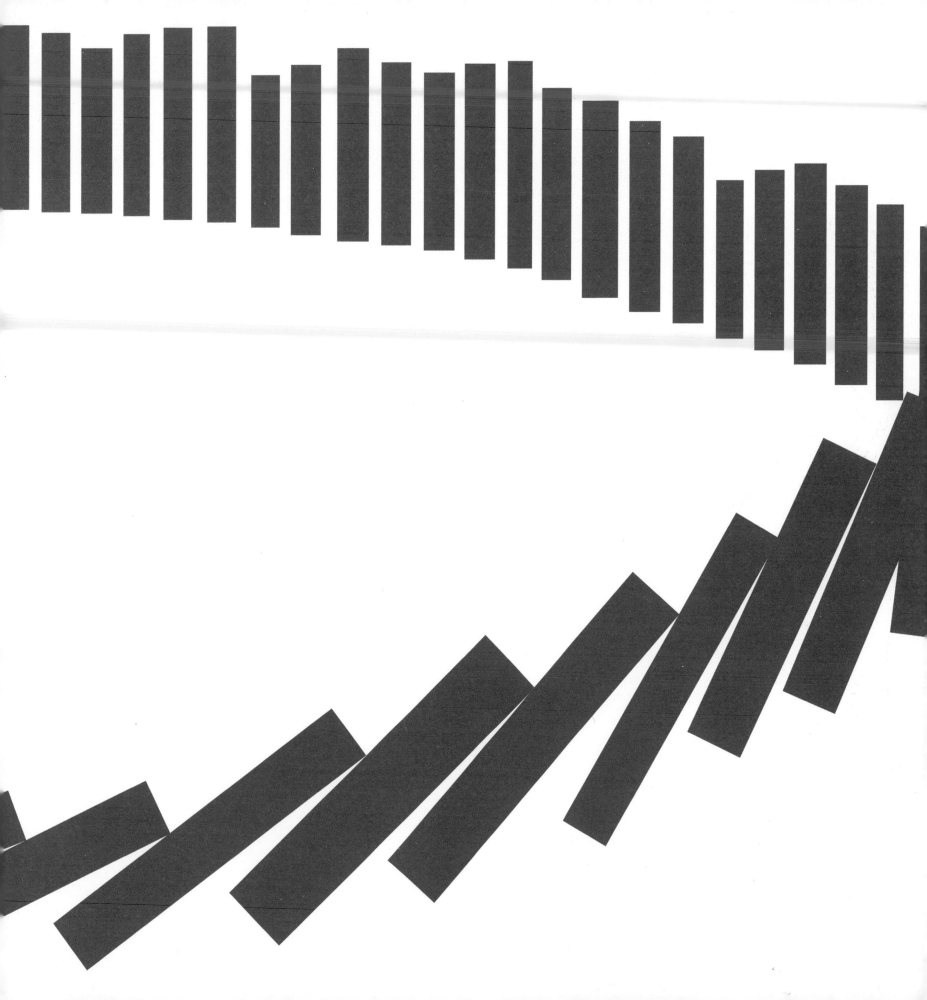

The **RED RECTANGLES** tried their best to defeat

the GREEN LIZARDS,

but the **GREEN LIZARDS** were strong.

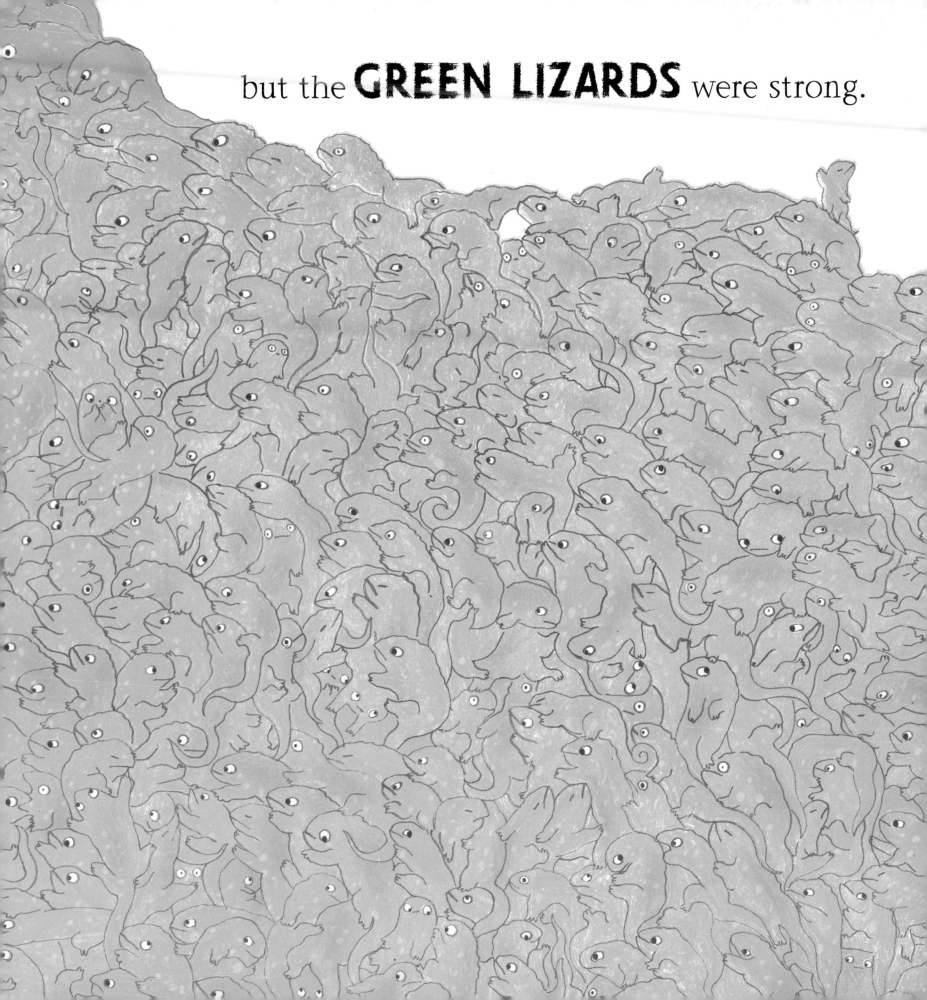

WHAT ARE WE FIGHTING FOR?

asked one **GREEN LIZARD.**

But he was SQUASHED, and this led to...

THE BIGGEST WAR EVER. They fought...

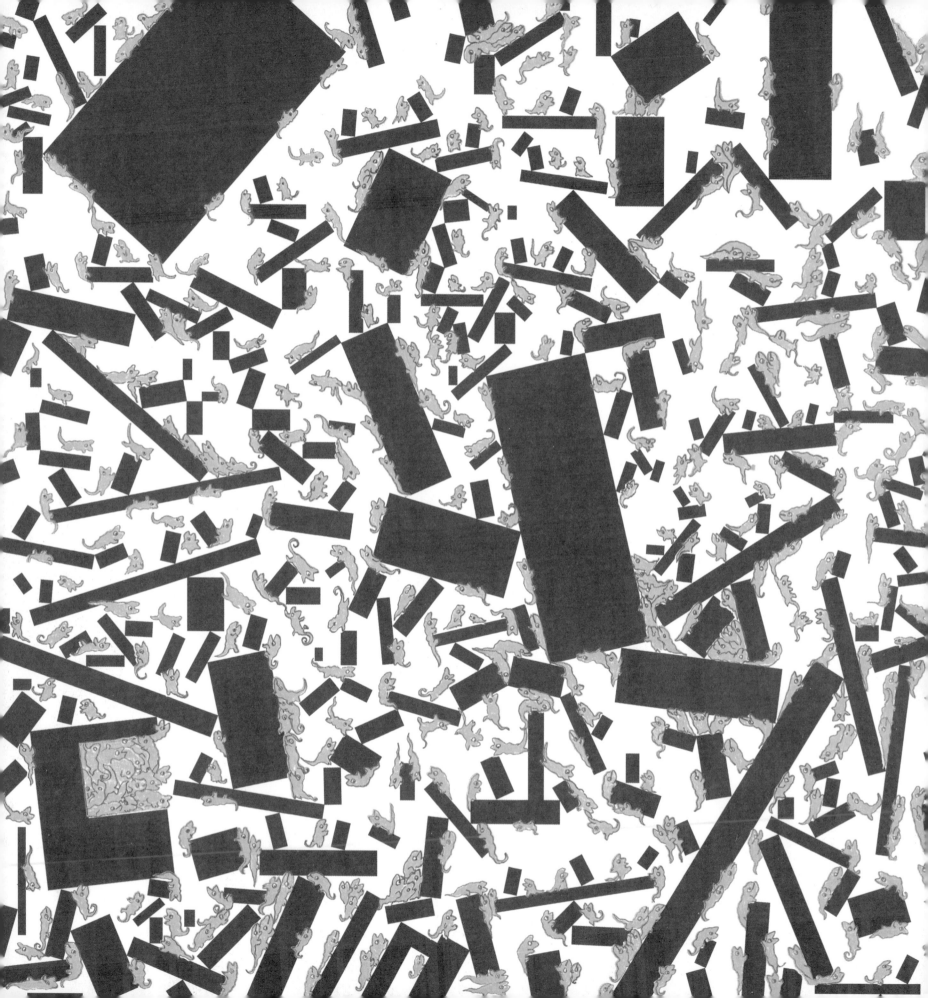

and fought and fought until...

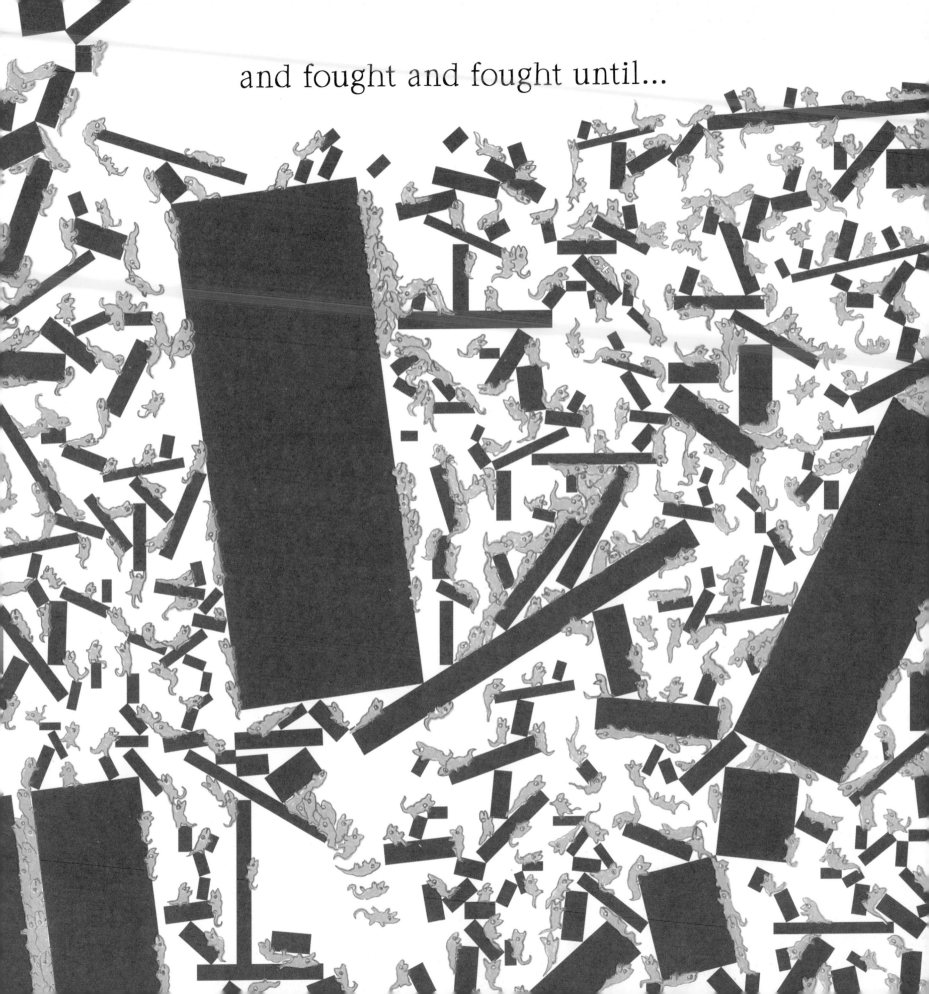

they could fight no more.

ENOUGH IS ENOUGH!

said one **RED RECTANGLE.**

The **GREEN LIZARDS** and the **RED RECTANGLES** gathered for a truce, and finally they found a way...

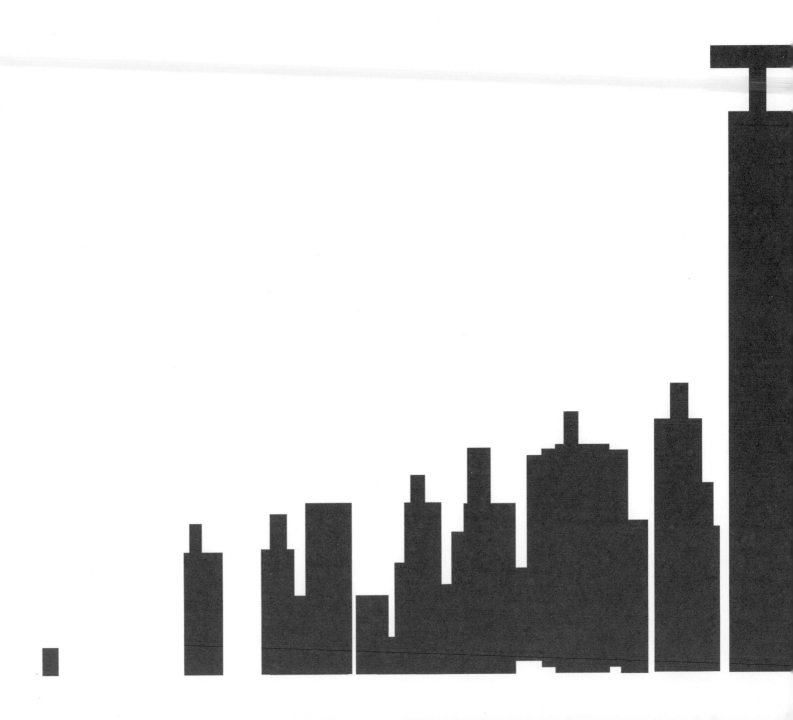

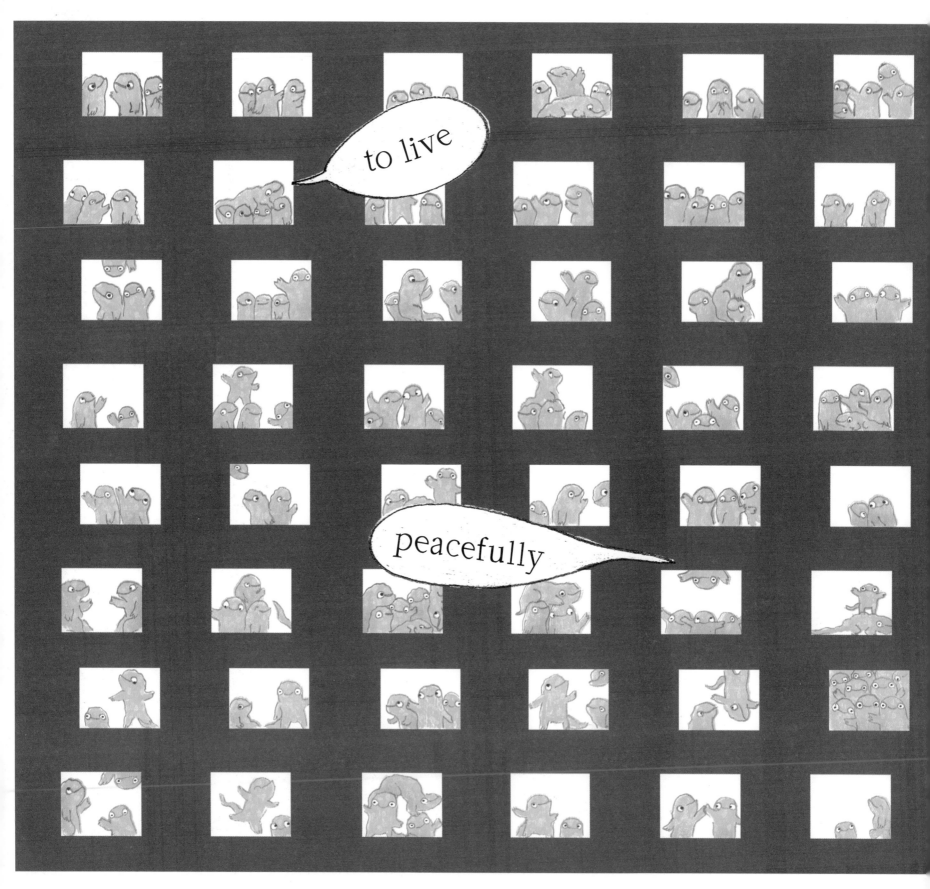

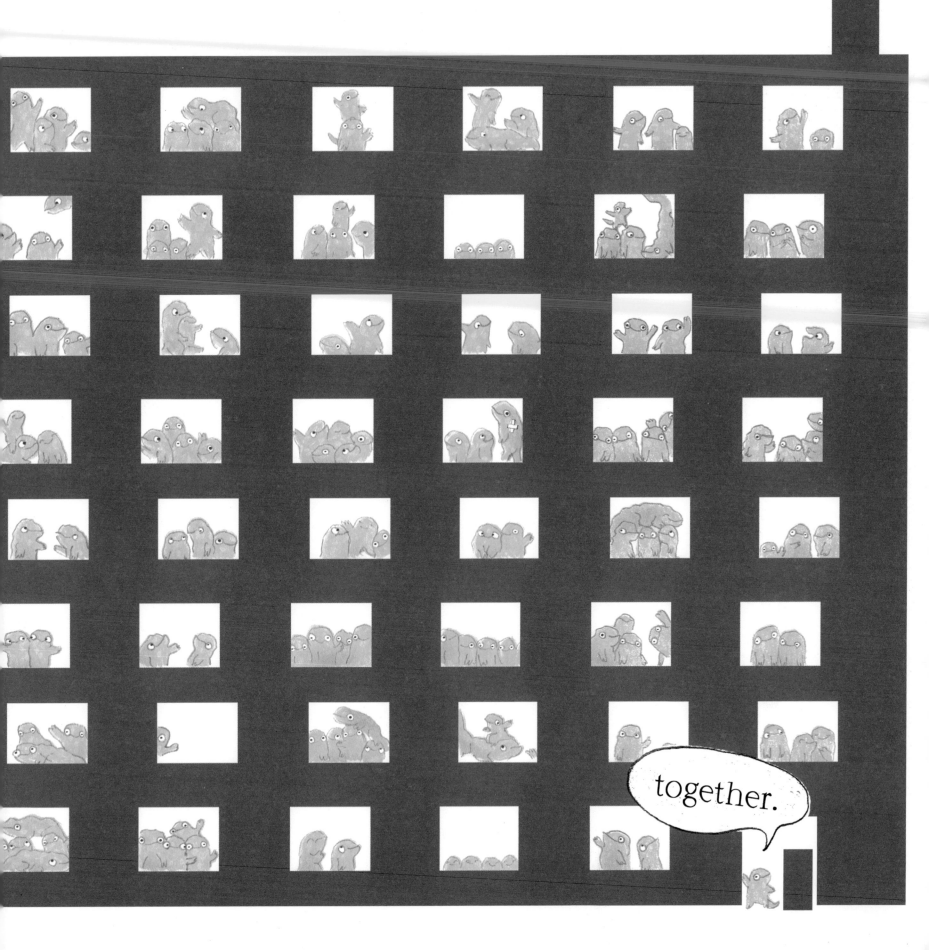